GRACE
STREET
KIDS

JOSH &
THE GUINEA PIG

GRACE STREET KIDS
Josh & THE GUINEA PIG

STANDARD
PUBLISHING
Cincinnati, Ohio

Marti Plemons

Grace Street Kids

Megan & the Owl Tree
Josh & the Guinea Pig
Georgie & the New Kid
Scott & the Ogre

Acquisition and editing by March Media, Inc.

The Standard Publishing Company, Cincinnati, Ohio.
A division of Standex International Corporation.

99 98 97 96 95 94 93 92   5 4 3 2 1

Library of Congress Cataloging-in-Publication Data

Plemons, Marti.
  Josh & the guinea pig / Marti Plemons.
    p. cm. — (Grace Street kids)
  Summary: Josh hates having to put up with his inconsiderate cousin Matt, who
has come to stay for the summer, until a competition to memorize Bible verses
brings him a new understanding about selfishness and jealousy.
  ISBN 0-87403-686-0
  [1. Cousins—Fiction. 2. Christian life—Fiction.] I. Title. II. Title: Josh and the
guinea pig. III. Series: Plemons, Marti. Grace Street kids.
    PZ7.P718Jo 1992
    [Fic]—dc20   91-40643
                                                      CIP
                                                      AC

For Nicholas

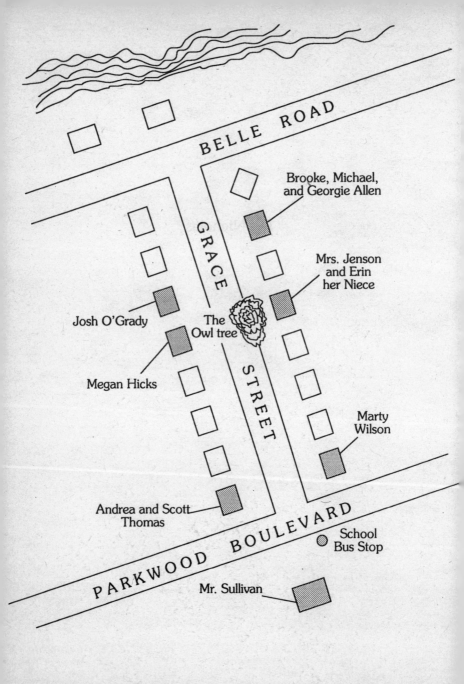

Chapter One

Josh woke up slowly. With his eyes still closed, he turned his face to the window and let the sunlight seep through his eyelids.

Outside, blue jays were creating a ruckus in the Owl Tree. Mrs. Jenson's cat was probably out again. Josh yawned widely and listened to the lazy ticktock of his Le Mans alarm clock. It didn't seem like Saturday. It seemed . . .

Josh's eyes flew open. In one swift motion he threw back the covers and jumped out of bed. It

wasn't Saturday. It was only Thursday. It was . . .
He grabbed the clock. It was after eight-thirty!
Why hadn't the alarm gone off? Why hadn't his
mom been in to get him up? He had missed the
bus. He was already late for school. It was terri-
ble. It was . . .

. . . the first day of summer vacation. Josh
laughed out loud and fell back onto the bed. The
alarm clock rolled from his fingers and hid its
face in the covers. No more school for three
whole months. No more sixth grade, ever! The
smell of bacon frying drifted through the door
and made his stomach growl. Josh dressed
quickly and hurried downstairs.

"Hello, sleepyhead."

"Hi, Mom." Josh went to the stove. He kissed
his mom's cheek while reaching around her to
steal a piece of bacon.

"How do you want your eggs?"

"Scrambled."

"Why do I ask?"

"I don't know." Josh always wanted his eggs
scrambled.

His mom laughed. "What are you going to do
today?"

Josh shrugged and waited. That question usually meant she had plans of her own for him.

"Well, sometime today I need you to clean your room and decide where you want Matt to put his things when he gets here."

"Why can't he stay in the guest room?"

"I thought he'd feel more comfortable if we put him in with you. You know he shares a room with his brother at home."

"So maybe he'd like to have his own room for a change."

"Don't argue, please."

Josh knew better than to say anything else, but he wasn't at all happy about giving up half his room to Matt Delaney. The last time Matt came to visit, he took Josh's bicycle without asking and tore up one of the wheels trying to jump the creek.

Matt's dad and Josh's mom were brother and sister. Uncle Marshall and Aunt Harriet lived three states away, where Josh wished Matt would stay. Aunt Harriet needed an operation, though, and Josh's mom had offered to take care of Matt while Aunt Harriet was in the hospital. But Matt wasn't even a whole year younger than

Josh. Josh thought that was plenty old enough for Matt to stay home alone with his older brother, Will.

"What's Will going to do?"

"He's working this summer, at a movie theater."

"Oh." Josh piled scrambled egg on the corner of a piece of toast and took a bite. He wouldn't have minded so much if Will were coming too. Will was four years older than Josh, but he let Josh hang out with him anyway, and Will was the only person Josh knew who was better than he was on a skateboard.

"Josh?"

Josh stopped in the middle of a drink of milk and looked at his mom. She came across the kitchen and sat down next to him.

"I want you to make a special effort to be nice to Matt while he's here."

"I'm nice. He's the one . . ."

"That's what I'm talking about. You'll have to make allowances. He's going to be worried about his mom."

The serious look on his mom's face frightened Josh. "Aunt Harriet will be OK, won't she?"

His mom gave him a smile. It was the one she used when Josh did something right. "She'll be fine," she said. "Will you promise to help by being extra nice to Matt?"

"Sure."

Josh endured a hug, then finished his milk. Five minutes later he was digging for Formula One race cars among the covers of his bed. He found six cars, a flatbed transport truck, and his alarm clock. He watched the little Le Mans car at the end of the second hand race around the tiny road pictured on the clock's face. Satisfied that the clock was still running, Josh returned it to its place on the nightstand.

Sitting between the twin beds, the nightstand was actually a rollaway metal tool chest enameled bright red. Josh used the shallow drawers to store his model cars. He loved cars. His dad said a good Irishman should love horses, but Josh loved cars.

Josh flipped the switch on the floor lamp in the corner. It looked like a miniature traffic light and flashed red, yellow, and green across the YIELD sign above his bed. He used to sleep in a bed that looked like a race car, but he outgrew that. Now he had two beds and Matt was going to use one of them. Josh looked at the other bed. A DO NOT ENTER sign covered the wall above it. There was a big red STOP sign on the door, too, but it wasn't going to keep Matt away.

Josh sighed. After he finished cleaning his room, he grabbed his skateboard and went outside. He sailed down the driveway and skidded to a noisy stop at the sidewalk. Across Grace Street, Mrs. Jenson was tiptoeing through the purple and yellow irises that grew alongside of her front porch. Suddenly she lunged. A flash of white fur streaked across the yard and disappeared around the far corner of the house.

Mrs. Jenson straightened up, brushing the black dirt from her hands. Spying Josh, she called, "Well, don't just stand there, Josh O'Grady! Come help me catch Mr. Peepers."

Josh groaned. He didn't even like Mrs. Jenson. All the other Grace Street Kids treated the old crow like she was their grandmother, or something. Josh thought she was mean, always yelling at him to keep his skateboard off her precious driveway. With a flip of his toe he sent the

skateboard into the edge of his yard and then trudged slowly across the street.

Mrs. Jenson hurried him. "Come on, Josh. He'll be in the next county by the time you get here!"

Josh picked up his speed to a slow jog and angled toward the garage. Mrs. Jenson turned and headed around the other side. If the cat was in the backyard, they would have him cornered. Josh pushed through the forsythia hedge and looked around the yard. Near the back fence was a small shed where Mrs. Jenson stored her gardening tools. Gazing out from between the snapdragons that stood single file around the base of the shed were two large blue eyes surrounded by a giant fluff of white fur.

Josh waved at Mrs. Jenson and pointed to the shed. Crouching low, he circled around the edge of the yard, being careful not to get too near the shed. Mr. Peepers hunched his shoulders and watched closely. By the time he realized there was someone else in the yard, Mrs. Jenson was upon him. She snatched him up and turned to Josh.

"That was very clever, Josh," she told him with a smile.

Josh shrugged.

"I've made a fresh batch of chocolate chip cookies. Would you like some?"

"Sure." Even if it was Mrs. Jenson, you just didn't turn down homemade chocolate chip cookies!

Mrs. Jenson brought the cookies and a pitcher of lemonade to the patio. "I was airing out Erin's room," she said, "and Mr. Peepers found the open window. It was careless of me. Thank goodness you were around to help catch him."

Josh studied the white rubber toes of his canvas high-tops.

Mrs. Jenson smiled and offered him another cookie. "Won't it be nice to have Erin back with us?"

"When's she coming?"

"Next week sometime. Her mother wasn't sure of the day."

Erin's mom was a surgical nurse in the city. She and Erin lived downtown in a high-rise apartment building. Josh thought summers in the city would be great, but every year Erin couldn't wait for school to be over so she could spend the summer in the Parkwood subdivision with Mrs. Jenson. She called her Aunt Jody.

"You're Erin's aunt, right?"

"I was her father's aunt. I'm Erin's great-aunt."

"Oh." Josh had trouble thinking of Mrs. Jenson as anyone's aunt. "So, she's coming next week?"

"Tuesday, maybe. It depends on her mother's schedule."

"My cousin's coming this Saturday."

"How nice!"

"Yeah, I guess. His mom's having an operation."

"Oh, I see. How long will he be staying?"

"A week, maybe. Maybe two."

"Well, you must bring him over so we can meet him."

"It's just Matt," said Josh.

"Oh, yes. I remember Matt." Mrs. Jenson tried to hide the look on her face, but Josh caught a glimpse of a frown before she turned away. *She doesn't like him either!* thought Josh. Maybe she wasn't such an old crow after all.

On Saturday, Josh went with his dad to the airport. They left early so they could stop off at the construction firm where his dad worked as an engineer. The door to his office said Patrick O'Grady in tiny gold letters. but everyone still called him Rusty like they used to when he worked on building sites running a backhoe. Josh ran his fingers through his own fiery red O'Grady hair. Sometimes people called him Red. He liked Rusty better.

"I'll be done in the blink of an eye, Josh, so don't you go prowling around."

"OK." Josh didn't much like the office on Saturdays, anyway. The people were gone, the machines were quiet, and the rooms were dark and lonely. When the rooms were full of people, they gave him snacks and let him play with the copier because he was Rusty's kid.

"Dad?"

"What?"

"Are we rich?"

Josh's dad threw back his head and laughed a deep, bellowing laugh. "Now why would you want to ask a thing like that?"

"Matt says we are."

"Does he, indeed?" His dad's green eyes sparkled. "And what do you say?"

Josh shrugged.

"Well, let me put it this way." His dad sat on the edge of the desk so he could look into Josh's eyes. "There're those that are worse off than we are, to be sure. But there're plenty that are better off, too. I'd say we were fortunate enough to be somewhere along about the middle."

"I told Matt we weren't rich," mumbled Josh.

"I don't know. From his point of view, maybe we are rich."

"You mean Uncle Marshall's poor?"

"I mean Uncle Marshall and Aunt Harriet haven't always had things as easy as we have." He rested his large, strong hands on Josh's shoulders. "You have to try to see things through Matt's eyes, son, or you'll never be able to get along with him. You understand?"

"I think so."

"Good. Now, let's go get your cousin."

Chapter Two

"Hello, O'Gradys!"

"Hello yourself, Delaney!" Josh's dad wrapped Matt in a bear hug.

"What's that?" asked Josh.

"You mean this?" Matt held up a white cardboard airline carrier. It had rows of quarter-sized holes all over it, and printed on each side were the words CAUTION, LIVE ANIMAL.

"Yeah. You got an animal in there?"

"It's just Widgett. She's a guinea pig."

"Mom won't let animals in the house."

Josh's dad winked at Matt. "Oh, I doubt that she'd mind just for a week or two. Come on, let's get your bags."

As they started off down the concourse, Matt gave Josh a triumphant smile. Ordinarily, the airport was one of Josh's favorite places. He loved watching the planes take off and land. He loved the crackly, official-sounding voice that announced their departures and arrivals. Josh liked to make up stories about the people he saw rushing to and from the flights. Now Matt was one of those people, and Josh couldn't even enjoy seeing the luggage riding the carousel like children on a merry-go-round.

"Race you to the car!" shouted Matt, who was halfway out the door before Josh could start his feet moving.

The car was in short-term parking near the terminal. Matt must have spotted it before he started running because he made a beeline for it and stood panting by the front passenger door by the time Josh finally got there.

"I win. I get to ride up front."

Josh frowned but was too out of breath to say anything. Matt was taller than Josh and his legs were longer, but Josh still thought he could have beaten him if the race had been fair. Matt put the guinea pig on the backseat with Josh.

"What'd you say his name was? Midget?"

"Widgett," said Matt. "and she's a girl."

"How can you tell?" Josh peered through one of the holes but couldn't see anything. When he looked up again, he saw a smile crinkled around his dad's eyes.

"The guy at the pet shop said so."

"Well, I don't want her in my room."

"Oh, come now, Josh," said his dad. "I suppose she's got a cage inside that box?" he asked Matt.

"'Course she has."

"There now, you see? She won't be giving you any trouble."

Josh wasn't so sure, but he didn't say any more about it. In fact, he didn't say much of anything the rest of the way home. He just moped in the backseat while his dad chatted with Matt about Uncle Marshall, Aunt Harriet, and Will. As soon as they were home Josh tried to escape on his skateboard, but his mom called him back.

"Go upstairs and help your cousin get settled in," she told him.

In my room, thought Josh as he slowly climbed the stairs. Matt had dumped his things in the middle of Josh's bed. "That's my bed," Josh told him.

"I like to sleep near the windows."

"So do I," said Josh and tossed Matt's suitcase onto the other bed. When he reached for the guinea pig, Matt grabbed it first. Josh watched as he opened the box and pulled out the cage. Inside it, ramps and ladders connected shelves in three corners. An exercise wheel stood in the center like a miniature Ferris wheel. The fourth corner contained a black and white ball of fur, partially hidden beneath a pile of cedar chips.

"She's sleeping," said Matt. "The vet gave her a pill."

"What kind of pill?"

"I don't know . . . a sleeping pill! So she wouldn't get sick on the airplane."

"Oh."

Matt put the cage on the desk and stood watching the sleeping guinea pig.

"So are you going to unpack, or what?" Josh asked.

Matt took his suitcase and slid it under his bed. "All done. What are we going to do now?"

Josh grabbed his skateboard. "I'm going to catch some board time before it gets dark. I don't care what you do."

"OK, I'll come with you." When Josh glared at him Matt added, "You said you didn't care."

Josh went outside by the front door so he wouldn't have to go through the kitchen and past his mom. Matt went through the kitchen. Josh was three houses down the street, expertly guiding his skateboard in and out of the sidewalk's curves, when Matt caught up with him on Josh's bike. Josh skidded to a stop.

"Who said you could ride my bike?"

"Your mom."

Josh sulked. "What do I care? I don't ever ride that old thing anyway."

"That's what your mom said."

Josh pushed off and rode the skateboard just a little too fast, taking the curves just a little too sharply. Matt kept up with him on the bicycle, riding in the street near the curb. At the end of

Grace Street Josh made a quick one-eighty, which
sent two wheels skidding off the curb and almost
tumbled Josh into the traffic on Parkwood
Boulevard.

"Hey, watch it!" shouted Matt.

"No problem," said Josh.

"You want to swap going back?"

"No."

"Come on, just back to your house."

"No!"

"Fine," said Matt. "I didn't want to ride your
stupid skateboard anyway."

"Yes you did, and it isn't stupid."

"Is so! Everything about you is stupid, even
your stupid sidewalks! Who ever heard of
squiggly sidewalks?"

"They're not squiggly. They're curvy."

"What's the difference? They're still stupid."

"They are not!"

"They're special," said Marty, walking up
behind them.

Marty Wilson lived on Grace Street at the
corner of Parkwood Boulevard, directly across
from where Josh and Matt had been shouting at
each other. She was younger than Josh and two

years behind him in school.

"This must be your cousin," she said.

"Yeah, that's Matt," said Josh.

"I'm Marty."

"Hi," grunted Matt, still sulking from the fight.

"Is Georgie home?" she asked Josh.

Georgie Allen was Marty's best friend and she lived across the street from Josh but almost at the other end of Grace Street.

"How should I know?"

Marty sighed. "Just tell me if their car was there."

"Yeah, I think so."

"Thanks. I would have called, but my mom was using the phone. See ya, Matt."

Marty angled back across the street and Josh shoved off up the sidewalk. Matt turned the bike, watched them both, and followed Marty up the street. Josh whipped past his house and looked across at the Allen house. Georgie's sister, Brooke, was sharing the porch swing with Megan Hicks.

Megan lived next door to Josh, across from Mrs. Jenson. When they were kids Megan drove him crazy. She liked frogs and snakes as much as he did. Megan was still a tomboy, but now Josh thought she was pretty cool.

Brooke waved at him. "Hey, Josh, come here a minute!"

Josh skimmed across the pavement and up to the porch rail. "Brooksie! Hiccu . . . uh . . . Megan! What's up?" Megan didn't like to be called Hiccups, and Josh was trying to remember that.

"Who's that with Marty?" asked Brooke.

"It's just my cousin."

"I told you it was Matt," said Megan.

"He's a lot cuter since the last time he was here."

"It's still Matt," Megan reminded her.

Josh watched Matt turn in the Allens' driveway, pedaling in slow motion to keep pace with Marty. "Hey, Mattress," he called, "who's your new girlfriend?"

"Shut up, Josh," said Marty.

Matt yelled, "Who are you calling Mattress?"

"Mattress Delaney," said Josh. "I guess that'd be you."

"Oh, yeah?" Matt pushed his face up close to Josh's and clenched his hands into fists at his side.

"Stop it!" shouted Megan.

Everyone was surprised into silence. Josh looked at Megan. Her face was nearly as red as his hair. Megan glared back at him. "What?" he asked innocently.

Megan threw up her hands and rolled her eyes. "Josh O'Grady! You're just . . . You're so . . ." she stammered.

"Stupid," said Matt.

"And the same goes double for you, Matt Delaney!"

"That's right," agreed Brooke. "And you, you, *boys* can just go home if you're going to act like that!"

Josh looked at Matt and shrugged. Together they headed for Josh's house.

"Girls!" said Matt.

"Yeah."

Chapter Three

Sundays were special at the O'Grady house. Josh's mom made pancakes or waffles for breakfast while Josh and his dad took turns reading the comics and the sports section of the city's thick newspaper. Then, dressed in what Grandma Delaney used to call *Sunday finery,* Josh and his dad would discuss batting averages or total yardage as the three of them drove to church.

Matt ruined everything. He complained that

he didn't like waffles and asked for cereal instead. He hogged the sports section and then he announced that he didn't go to church.

"That's not the truth now, is it Matthew?" asked Josh's dad sternly. "Fine Christians that your folks are, not going to church?"

"They go."

"And they'd want you to go, too," said Josh's mom.

"But they don't make me, if I don't want to."

"I'm sorry you don't want to go, son," said Mr. O'Grady, "but in this house we go to church. All of us." he added firmly.

Matt made jokes and picked at Josh all during Sunday school and sulked through the worship service. Josh wanted to move across the aisle and pretend he didn't have a cousin. On the way home he asked, "You're not going to make him go to Bible school next week, are you?"

His dad sighed and looked at his mom. "I suppose not," she said, "if he's that set against it."

"Good."

Matt said, "What if I *want* to go to Bible school?"

"That would be great," said Josh's mom.

"Yeah, great," said Josh sarcastically.

"Josh . . ." warned his dad.

"Well, he only wants to go because I don't want him to."

"Liar!"

"Matthew Jonathan Delaney!" Josh's mom whipped her head around to the backseat. "Didn't either of you hear a word that was said in church today?"

"I did," said Josh quickly.

"So did I," said Matt. "It was about Joseph."

"And did you understand that it was out of jealousy that his brothers sold him into slavery?"

"But he had the last laugh," said Josh, "because it made him rich and famous."

"No, Josh," said his mom, "it didn't. It was God who made something good from a bad situation, and it was Joseph's faith in God."

"That's what I meant," mumbled Josh.

Matt snickered.

"Nothing good comes from jealousy, and I don't want to see any more of it between the two of you. Is that clear?"

Josh looked at his hands. "Yes."

His mom looked at Matt. "And no more name calling?"

"Yes. I mean no."

Josh grinned at Matt's confusion. He couldn't help it. He knew his mom was right, that God didn't like the way he felt about Matt. He was going to try to do better, too, but the grin just slipped out. As soon as Josh's mom turned back around in her seat, Matt punched Josh on the arm.

When they got home, Josh chased Matt upstairs. Matt ran to Josh's room and tumbled onto the nearest bed. Josh stopped at the door. Matt's clothes were hanging from the traffic-light lamp. All his shoes were strewn about the floor—all except the one that scattered Josh's collection of baseball cards when it landed on the bottom shelf of the bookcase above the desk.

Widgett hopped into her exercise wheel and started running. Josh frowned. In the middle of the night Widgett's pill had worn off and he had been awakened by the squeak-rattle of that wheel.

"Why does she keep doing that?"

Matt sat up and smiled at the guinea pig. "She wants me to notice her."

"Well, say hi or something so she'll stop that racket."

Matt went to the desk and reached through the trapdoor at the top of the cage. Widgett scampered to his hand. He pulled her up and held her out to Josh. "Isn't she cool?"

Josh looked at the shiny black eyes and the long fur that stuck out in every direction, like Josh's hair when he first got up in the morning. He said, "She's OK, I guess," and he went to the closet to change out of his Sunday clothes. Matt didn't need to change. He had worn jeans to church.

After lunch, Josh returned to his room for his skateboard. He went to his desk to sneak another look at the guinea pig, but the trapdoor was still open and Widgett wasn't in her cage. Josh figured she was with Matt. As he turned to leave, though, a flake of cardboard drifted down and rested on the back of his hand. Josh looked up. On the top shelf of the bookcase, Widgett was busy shredding baseball cards to make a nest in Matt's shoe.

"Matt!" Josh snatched the card she was working on. She had nibbled off Darryl Strawberry's right ear and most of his Mets cap. "Matt!"

"What?" Matt ran into the room followed by Josh's mom.

"Look what she did!" roared Josh, holding out the chewed card.

"What's she doing out of her cage?" asked his mom. Widgett sat up and looked at them.

Matt took her carefully into his hands. "She needed some exercise."

Josh's mom frowned at Matt. "I won't have that animal roaming loose in this house," she told him. "Is that understood?"

Matt nodded. Josh waited. His mom smoothed the rough fur around the guinea pig's face. "You've been a bad girl," she said gently.

"Is that it?" demanded Josh. "What about my baseball cards?"

"What's done is done, Josh," said his mom.

"But—"

"We'll get you some more."

Josh grabbed his skateboard and stormed outside.

On Tuesday, Erin came. Josh was practicing

figure eights in the driveway when her mom's small, red car pulled in at Mrs. Jenson's house. He sailed across the street and up Mrs. Jenson's driveway, arriving just as Erin stepped out.

"Hi, Josh."

"Hi."

"Josh O'Grady!" Mrs. Jenson came charging across the porch. "How many times do I have to ask you to keep that thing off my driveway?"

"Sorry." Josh picked up the skateboard and held it under his arm.

Erin ran to hug Mrs. Jenson. "It's my fault, Aunt Jody. He came over to see me. Don't be mad at Josh."

Mrs. Jenson smiled at her niece. "I'm not angry," she said, then looked at Josh. "Would you like to come inside with us?"

"No, thanks," mumbled Josh, backing away.

"See you later," said Erin.

"See ya." Josh stood by the huge oak at the edge of Mrs. Jenson's yard until they had gone inside. Then he looked up into its branches. Megan Hicks looked back at him.

"How did you know I was up here?"

Josh shrugged. "Why didn't you come down?"

"I wanted to watch you get yelled at."

Josh dropped the skateboard to the sidewalk and rocked it back and forth with the toe of his sneaker. "It's just a driveway." he said. "Cars drive on it. What's she got against skateboards?"

"They tear up the concrete when you go off the edge."

"I don't go off the edge."

"Yes you do."

Josh sulked. He hated it when Megan was right, and she almost always was.

"Where's Matt?"

"I don't know and I don't care."

"Oh."

Josh looked thoughtfully at Mrs. Jenson's house. "You think she likes him?"

"Who?"

"Mrs. Jenson. I don't think she likes Matt."

"Mrs. Jenson likes everybody."

"She doesn't like me."

"Yes she does."

Josh looked up at Megan. "She does?"

"Sure. She just doesn't like your skateboard."

Josh ducked his head so Megan wouldn't see him smile. He wasn't sure why, but it made him happy to know that Mrs. Jenson liked him. Suddenly, more than ever, he wanted to think that she didn't like Matt. "She frowned when I said Matt was coming."

"She was probably remembering how he smashed the plants on her porch the last time he was here."

Josh *had* forgotten. Matt had been showing off, trying to walk the porch railing, when his foot slipped and he fell into a stepladder full of geraniums. "She sure was mad," he remembered. "She wouldn't even let us help her clean it up."

"Here he comes," said Megan.

Josh turned around. Matt was crossing the street. "What are you doing just standing there?" he asked Josh.

"He's talking to me," said Megan.

Matt looked up into the tree. "Oh, hi, Megan. Want to see my guinea pig?"

Matt held Widgett out for inspection. Megan dropped to the ground beside him. "It's so cute!" she squealed.

"Her name's Widgett."

"That midget pig's supposed to be in her cage," said Josh.

"Your mom said she couldn't be loose in the house," Matt countered. "She didn't say I couldn't take her outside."

"Let's go show her to Erin," said Megan, taking Widgett and starting toward Mrs. Jenson's house.

"Good idea," said Josh, "and introduce her to Mr. Peepers while you're there."

Megan hesitated. "Oh, yeah, I forgot."

"Who's Mr. Peepers?" asked Matt.

"Mrs. Jenson's cat."

"A very hungry cat," said Josh, "who likes to eat midget pigs!"

"He does not," said Megan, then frowned. "At least, I don't think he does."

"Let's go find out." Josh reached for the guinea pig but Matt grabbed her first.

"No!"

"He was only kidding," said Megan.

"Oh."

Josh grinned. Matt's face was turning red. He had really believed Josh was going to feed Widgett to Mr. Peepers. "Don't be so stupid," Josh told him.

"I'm not stupid. I know you don't like Widgett."

"She ate my baseball cards!"

"Did not! She just shredded a couple."

"OK, she *shredded* my baseball cards, but I guess I can put up with her for a couple of weeks."

Suddenly Matt smiled. "Oh, I forgot to tell you!"

"What?" asked Josh, dreading the answer.

"My dad called a while ago."

"How's your mom?" asked Megan.

"Not so good. I mean, she's going to be OK and everything. It's just going to take longer than they figured for her to get better."

"How much longer?" asked Josh.

"A couple of months," said Matt. Then he smiled wickedly at Josh. "I get to stay the whole summer!"

Chapter Four

B ut, Mom . . ."
"Josh, you promised you'd be nice to Matt."

"For two weeks, not for the whole summer!"

"For heaven's sake, Josh, he's your cousin. He's family."

"But it's *my* birthday."

"Josh, that's enough. He's going to your party and that's all there is to it."

Josh couldn't believe it. It was like his worst

nightmare. He was stuck with Matt for the entire summer, and his mom was going to see to it that Matt was included in everything Josh did. He didn't even *want* a birthday party if Matt had to be there, but he knew better than to tell his mom that. Josh picked up his skateboard and went outside. Matt was sitting on the back steps next to the open door.

"You spying on me, Matt?"

"No."

"Well, just don't."

"I wasn't."

Josh hesitated. He hadn't really meant for Matt to know that he didn't want him at the party. He felt that he ought to say something, but he didn't know what. Finally, he dropped his skateboard to the concrete and started down the driveway.

The other kids were over at Erin's, so Josh left the skateboard on the edge of his yard and walked across the street. Marty was sitting in the porch swing between Erin and Georgie. Brooke was on the railing, propped against a post. Even Michael Allen was there, sprawled out on the steps.

Michael was the middle Allen, younger than

Brooke and older than Georgie. He stayed inside a lot, and when he did hang out with the kids he never said much. Josh liked him. When Josh came across the yard, Michael moved over so he could sit beside him.

"Where's Megan?"

"Softball," said Brooke.

"Oh, yeah." In addition to climbing trees and liking frogs, Megan played softball all summer long.

"Where's Matt?" asked Brooke.

"Home, I guess," said Josh. But as he spoke, a familiar sound reached his ears. It was the grinding of skateboard wheels on concrete. Matt was careening down the sidewalk in front of Megan's house—on Josh's skateboard!

Josh jumped to his feet. "Matt!"

"He's not very good, is he?" said Michael.

"Matt!" shouted Josh, and ran after him. Michael was right. Matt was barely keeping the board on the sidewalk, and when he got to Parkwood Boulevard, his attempt at a one-eighty spin sent him flying onto the grass near the curb. The skateboard shot into the path of a blue and white truck from the city's sanitation department. The driver honked angrily as the big truck crushed the board beneath its wheels.

Josh stared. "My skateboard," he said softly.

"There was something wrong with it, anyway," said Matt, dusting off the seat of his jeans. "The wheels locked or something. It threw me off."

"You killed my skateboard," said Josh, still staring at its tangled wheels and broken back.

"Sorry, man, but the wheels . . ." Matt began, but stopped when Josh turned on him.

"You had no right! It was mine!"

"I said I was sorry."

"*Sorry* doesn't get my skateboard back, does it?"

"It wasn't my fault. The wheels . . ."

Josh shoved Matt and walked away. He wanted to punch his lights out, but he could just imagine what his mother would say if she found out they were fighting. Watching for traffic, he picked up the pieces of his skateboard and carried them back to Erin's porch. The kids gathered around him.

"Josh," said Erin worriedly, "your skateboard."

"Is Matt OK?" asked Brooke.

Michael poked her in the ribs and gave her a dirty look.

"What are you going to do?" Marty asked.

"I don't know," said Josh. "I can't kill him. He's family."

"Maybe we could hire somebody," said Michael earnestly.

Josh looked at him closely and saw just the trace of a smile in his dark eyes. Josh grinned. "Yeah. Anybody know a good hit man?" The others laughed. "How about you, Erin? You live in the city."

"I'm sorry, Josh," said Erin.

"That's OK."

"About your skateboard, I mean."

"Yeah, I know."

When Josh showed his parents the remains of the skateboard, his father patted him on the back and left the room. His mom grabbed Matt by the shoulders. "Are you all right?" she asked anxiously. "You could have been killed!"

"What about my skateboard?" demanded Josh.

"This was going to be your birthday present," said his dad, coming back into the room. He was carrying the brand-new skateboard Josh had been hinting for since before Christmas.

Josh whooped. "All right!" He took the skateboard and lovingly checked out every inch of it. "Thanks, Dad." He kissed his mom. "Thanks, Mom."

Matt beamed. "See there? Everything worked out just fine."

"Not so fast there, Matthew," said Josh's dad. "You had no business taking that skateboard without asking Josh."

"And I don't want either of you playing hear Parkwood Boulevard anymore," said his mom. "There's far too much traffic."

"But, Mom . . ."

"I mean it, Josh. You'll stay on this end of Grace Street or you'll not ride that thing at all."

"Dad?"

"You heard your mother, son."

"Yes, sir."

"And, Matt, you're not to be taking off with Josh's things without his permission."

"Yes, sir."

"Now, that's an end to it. Is that clear?"

Matt nodded. Josh glared at Matt.

"Josh?"

"Yes, sir."

Josh took the new skateboard up to his room. Matt followed him. "Aren't you going to try it out?"

"Later," said Josh. "Right now I have to murder a midget pig."

Matt's mouth tried to grin, but his eyes looked worried. "You're kidding, right?"

"Right," said Josh. "I'd rather murder you."

"Your dad said it's over, remember? Anyway, you got a new skateboard, so it doesn't matter."

"Yeah? Well, the laugh's on you, isn't it? If you hadn't smashed the old one, you could have ridden it after I got this one. Now, you're just out of luck."

"I don't care. There was something wrong with it, anyway."

"The only thing wrong was the person riding it."

"The wheels locked up!"

"Oh, shut up, Matt. We both know that's not true."

Matt looked away. Josh thought for a minute that Matt was going to cry. Instead, he went to the desk and took Widgett from her cage. Josh almost felt sorry for him.

"It's OK if you go to my party," Josh told him.

"You think I care about your old party?"

"I guess not," said Josh, "but if you *did* want to go, it would be OK."

The party was held Friday afternoon in the video arcade of a local pizza place. All the Grace Street Kids were there, including the youngest, Georgie and Marty. Josh's mom said he couldn't invite Brooke and Michael without inviting Georgie, and Josh knew he couldn't ask Georgie without asking Marty. He didn't mind, though. Josh's rule of birthdays was, *the more people you invite, the more presents you get!* And Josh got lots of presents.

The Allens gave him a dozen new race cars. Erin gave him a T-shirt from the city zoo. A black panther stalked across the front, and the zoo's familiar logo decorated the back. Marty gave him an old Indy 500 infield pass.

Stunned, Josh asked, "How'd you get this?"

"My grandpa works for a newspaper in Indianapolis, and he took us to the race one year."

"And you went to the pits?"

"Yeah. It was real noisy."

"Noisy? Marty . . ." Josh stopped, speechless. He would have given his brand-new skateboard for a chance like that, and Marty just thought it was "noisy."

"Don't you like it? I asked Grandpa to send a poster, but it didn't get here yet. Dad said you'd like the pass even better."

"Marty, it's great!"

"Oh! Well, good. You can still have the poster when it comes."

"Thanks. Really!"

Megan gave him baseball cards, replacing everything Widgett had shredded except the Darryl Strawberry. Then Matt handed him a small package and said, "Your dad gave me the money." It was a new Darryl Strawberry rookie card.

The pizza place gave them tokens for free video games, and they played for about an hour. Matt was really pretty good. Josh could almost have been proud of him, if he hadn't bragged so much about it. When Michael finally clobbered him at Ninja Turtles, Josh couldn't help feeling glad.

"It wasn't fair," complained Matt. "We don't have that one at home."

"Yeah, right," said Josh sarcastically.

"We don't!"

Josh's dad stepped between them and declared the party over. Josh gathered up his presents and thanked everyone for coming. His mom and dad had both driven to the pizza place, and Josh made sure he and Matt were in different cars going back. At home, though, Matt followed Josh upstairs and watched as he made room in the nightstand for his new race cars.

"Nice cars," said Matt.

"Yeah."

Matt sat down on the edge of his bed, next to the nightstand. "Can I see one?"

"No."

Matt just sat there, watching Josh. Josh tried to ignore him by studying the cars. He like the careful detail of the tiny steering wheels and miniature tires. He liked to feel the weight of the metal in the palm of his hand. They were pretty sturdy, he figured. Even Matt couldn't tear them up.

"OK," he said, handing Matt one of the cars.

Matt took it carefully and cradled it tenderly in his hand. Widgett's exercise wheel began to squeak-rattle furiously. Josh laughed. "I think she's jealous!"

When Matt looked at the guinea pig, she hopped out of the wheel, stood up against the side of her cage, and whistled at him. "I think you're right." He handed the car back to Josh and went to get Widgett.

Josh followed him. "Can I hold her?"

Matt put the guinea pig in Josh's hands. She wiggled herself around and gave Josh a curious look. Then she purred. "She likes you," said Matt.

Josh liked her, too. He didn't even care how silly he looked, standing there grinning at a guinea pig.

Chapter Five

Josh always looked forward to Bible school. He liked seeing the church kids every single day for a whole week, and he liked learning about the Bible, too. When he was little, his teachers told him stories of great battles and horrible plagues and how God had performed miracles to save His chosen people. And the stories about Jesus were even better. There were plots and murders and dead people coming back to life. Jesus had spies in His organization, and just when the bad guys thought they had won, He showed up again for a happy ending.

Now that Josh was older, he was learning how the stories could help him make decisions about his own life.

"The Bible is like an owner's manual," said Mr. Sparks.

"Like the user's guide to my dad's computer," suggested Josh.

"Exactly," agreed Mr. Sparks. "That's why it's important for you to learn as much about the Bible as you can. Now, who can recite a verse from memory? Any verse. Josh?"

"For God so loved the world that he gave his one and only Son, that whoever believes in him shall not perish but have eternal life," quoted Josh. "John 3:16."

"Very good," said Mr. Sparks and handed Josh a round, blue chip with a picture of a dove on one side and an open Bible on the other. "You'll get one chip for each new verse you learn this week," he explained. "On Friday, you can cash your chips in for prizes."

Everyone cheered.

"But there's a catch," said Mr. Sparks. The

cheers turned to groans. "Every day you'll have to recite all the verses you've learned before you can give us a new one."

Josh didn't mind. He was good at memorizing. He would learn a ton of verses and get more chips than anyone else.

"OK, who's next?" asked Mr. Sparks.

Matt raised his hand and Mr. Sparks nodded at him. "For God so loved the world," he quoted, "that he gave his one and only Son, that whoever believes in him shall not perish but have eternal life. John 3:16."

"That's the same one Josh gave us." said Mr. Sparks.

"You didn't say it had to be a different one," countered Matt.

Josh glared. "Cut it out, Matt," he warned. "That doesn't count."

"Yes, it does. He didn't say it had to be different!"

"Anybody knows you can't—"

"No, wait a minute, Josh," said Mr. Sparks. "Looks like he's got me on a technicality."

Mr. Sparks handed Matt a chip and Josh mumbled, "Cheater."

"Am not!"

Mr. Sparks ignored Matt's outburst and frowned at Josh. Then he turned to the rest of the class and asked, "Does anyone have a *different* verse to share with us?"

During recreation Josh cornered Matt behind the refreshment table. "You'd better knock it off," he told him.

"I didn't do anything."

"You cheated and you know it," said Josh. "Guess you don't think you can win if you play fair and square."

"I can win! I can learn more verses than you!"

"Yeah, if you cheat."

"I don't cheat."

"Well, we'll just see about that, won't we?"

On Tuesday, Matt earned three more chips. Josh quoted the Twenty-third Psalm and got chips for six new verses.

"Now who's cheating?" demanded Matt.

"You're just mad because you didn't think of it."

On Wednesday, Matt said the Lord's Prayer for five new verses. Someone else used one of Josh's before it was his turn, so he could only add two.

On Thursday, Josh got to go first, and he recited the entire thirteenth chapter of 1 Corinthians, all thirteen verses. When it was Matt's turn, he only added, "Jesus wept. John 11:35."

"That's it?" asked Josh.

"I was going to do the Love Chapter, too."

Josh smiled. He had him. He was twelve chips ahead, with just one day to go. There was no way Matt could catch up. Josh was so sure that he only added one new verse on Friday.

"Do to others as you would have them do to you," he quoted. "Luke 6:31. It's the Golden Rule."

"Yes, it is," said Mr. Sparks, "and it gives you a total of twenty-three verses!" The class applauded as he wrote the total on a chart and gave Josh another chip.

Josh was eight verses ahead of the person with the next highest total, but Matt was grinning at him. Josh didn't like it. He tried to think of what Matt could have. The Beatitudes, maybe, but that would only give him nine new verses, enough for second place but not enough to win.

Matt went last. After reciting all his previous verses, he smiled triumphantly at Josh and began quoting Genesis 1. Suddenly Josh wished *he* had used the Beatitudes instead of the Golden Rule. If Matt got through all six days of the Creation, Josh was sunk.

Mr. Sparks opened his Bible and followed along as Matt recited. Josh slid lower in his seat with each verse. After the third day, though, Matt tripped up on the creation of day and night, and Mr. Sparks stopped him. Josh sat up straight and waited.

"Excellent, Matt," said Mr. Sparks. "That was very impressive!"

Matt beamed and asked, "How many verses did I get?"

"Well, let's see." Mr. Sparks checked his Bible. "You added thirteen, so that gives you twenty-three. Looks like we have a tie!"

The class applauded. Josh scowled. He hated ties. It was like *nobody* won. It wasn't until after recreation, when Mr. Sparks had put out books and tapes and posters for them to spend their chips on, that Josh remembered the first chip Matt had won.

"You cheated for it," he told Matt. "That makes me the real winner."

"Does not, because I didn't cheat!"

They were still bickering when Josh's mom picked them up at noon. After they argued through lunch, she sent them to Josh's room and told them to stay there until she said they could come out.

"*Now* look what you did," grumbled Josh.

"Me? You're the one making trouble because you're such a sore loser!"

"I didn't lose!"

"Well, neither did I!"

Josh plopped on his bed and fumed in silence. He was tired of arguing. Matt was just plain stubborn. Josh watched him take Widgett from her cage. She squirmed excitedly in his hands until he lifted her to his shoulder where she snuggled against his neck. *Stupid guinea pig,* thought Josh. If *he* were allowed to have a pet, it would be a dog, not some stupid midget pig! But his mom wouldn't let a dog in the house, and his dad said there was too much traffic on the street to have one outside.

Josh sat up when his mom came into the room. "At least you've stopped arguing," she said. "You two have learned forty-six Bible verses this week and not one word has soaked into your heads!"

Josh looked at Matt, who was looking at the floor, and mumbled, "Forty-five."

His mom frowned at him. "Josh, get your Bible and look up James 3:16. When you find it, I want you to read it aloud." She consulted a piece of notepaper and turned to Matt. "Matt, you can be looking up Matthew 23:12."

Josh read, "For where you have envy and selfish ambition, there you find disorder and every evil practice."

His mom nodded. "Matt?"

Matt read, "For whoever exalts himself will be humbled; and whoever humbles himself will be exalted."

"Good. Now, I want you to spend the afternoon thinking about those verses. At supper I'll expect you each to explain what your verse means. Understood?"

Matt nodded. Josh said, "Do we have to stay in my room?"

"No. You can go outside, if you like. Maybe some sunshine will put the two of you in a better mood."

Josh wrote his verse on a piece of paper, stuck it in his pocket, and grabbed his new skateboard to go outside. Matt followed him out and walked over to Mrs. Jenson's where Erin was French-braiding Georgie's hair. Josh went looking for Megan. He found her in a tree by the creek, which ran behind the houses on Belle Road, at the end of Grace Street.

"What are you doing?"

"Just listening," she said. "What are you doing?"

"Nothing. Listening to what?"

"The creek."

"Oh."

Josh sat on his skateboard and rested his back against the tree. Megan climbed down easily and sat on the ground beside him. The creek gurgled and cooed like a happy baby. Josh had played in the creek plenty of times, but he had never simply listened to it.

"It's nice," he said.

"Yeah."

Josh looked around. "Where's Brooke?"

"Dance class."

Josh was glad. He liked talking to Megan, but

not when Brooke was around. He didn't think Brooke liked him very much. Reaching into his back pocket, he pulled out the slip of paper he had written his Bible verse on.

"What's that?" asked Megan.

"Just a verse." He handed her the paper.

"What's it for?"

"I'm supposed to think about it."

"Oh, yeah," said Megan, "you had Bible school this week. Ours isn't until next month."

Josh decided to let her think it was an assignment from Bible school. "So what do you think it means?"

Megan looked at the verse again. "I guess it means being jealous is a pretty bad thing."

"Guess so. What about that 'selfish ambition' part?"

"Well, *selfish* we know, and *ambition* means wanting things, so it must be wanting things just for yourself."

"Like not ever thinking about anybody else?"

"Or maybe it's wanting to have things your way all the time."

"Yeah, maybe."

"Anyway, it's bad."

"Yeah."

"I mean real bad."

"Why?"

"It says 'every evil practice.' That means if you start out being jealous, you could wind up doing just about anything!"

"It says all that?" Josh took the slip of paper and looked at the verse again.

At supper, Josh explained his verse using Megan's ideas. His mom smiled and his dad winked at him. "I think you've got it," he said. "Matthew? Let's hear yours."

Matt read his verse and said, "I guess it means *don't show off.*" He spoke the last three words at Josh.

"It's talking about pride, Matt," said Josh's mom.

"What's wrong with pride?" asked Josh.

"Nothing's wrong with pride, if it doesn't puff you up and it lets you admit you're hurting or that you need help," she told him.

"Oh." Josh thought he understood, but he wasn't sure.

His mom laughed. "OK," she said, "you're off the hook. Who wants dessert?"

"I'm not pass up dessert," said Josh's dad with a wink, "but I'll not let you off the hook just yet, either. It's my understanding that you boys tied at memorizing Bible verses."

It wasn't really a question, but Josh knew his dad was waiting for an answer. He nodded, deciding it wasn't a good time to bring up the part where Matt cheated.

"Well, that won't do," said his dad. "I think we should continue the contest until one of you wins. What do you think?"

Josh looked at Matt. Matt shrugged. Josh said, "I dare you."

"Fine with me," said Matt.

"All right," said Josh's dad, "new rules. One verse a day, and I'll tell you which one. We'll start with the two we've just talked about."

"Do we still have to say all the old ones every time?" asked Josh.

His dad nodded. "Including the Bible school verses. Agreed?"

"Agreed," said Josh, grinning at Matt. Matt would have to go through three days of the creation every single time.

Matt grinned back. "Agreed."

Chapter Six

"It's your turn, Josh."

"... disorder and every evil practice," said Josh.

"What?"

"What?" repeated Josh. All the Grace Street Kids were staring at him. They were in Megan's backyard, sitting on the hardwood yard gym their dads had built two summers ago. Mr. Hicks had bought the kit from a lumber yard and then invited everyone to a cookout and building party.

68

"It's your turn," said Erin.

"Oh." They were playing What If? and every-one was waiting for him to say something. "To ask, or to answer?"

Brooke rolled her eyes. "Josh! If you're going to play, you have to pay attention!"

"What were you thinking about?" asked Erin.

Every evil practice, thought Josh. He couldn't *stop* thinking about it. It had been almost a week since his dad started the verse contest. He had learned five new verses since his mom had made him explain the one from the book of James, but those three words kept hanging around in his head.

"Nothing," said Josh.

"Then ask us a What If? or pass," demanded Brooke. "You're holding up the game."

"I've got one," said Matt.

Matt was sitting apart from the group, on the railroad ties that framed a small sandbox. He had been digging trenches in the sand for Widgett instead of playing the game. They all turned to look at him.

"What if you want someone to like you, but they don't?"

"What if you want to like someone, but they keep doing stupid things so you can't?" Josh countered.

"No fair, Josh," said Brooke. "We already have a question."

"It was Josh's turn," Megan reminded her, "and I would just talk to them. You know, tell them how I felt."

"Maybe they can't help doing stupid things," said Michael.

"Maybe they're trying too hard," suggested Erin.

"Like dancing," agreed Brooke. "If you think too much about it, you can't do it."

Georgie laughed. "Is that why you're so good at it?"

Brooke poked her with a toe.

"I agree with Megan," Marty said. "If I really wanted to be friends, I would tell them."

"Me, too," said Georgie. "Then maybe they'd quit doing all the stupid stuff."

"This is a stupid game if you ask me," said Matt as he picked up Widgett and left.

"What's wrong with him?" asked Brooke.

Josh watched Matt stalk across the yard and

the words *every evil practice* nagged at him. "It's my fault," he said.

"What?"

"We all did it," said Megan.

"What?"

"Don't be so dense, Brooke," said Michael.

"I guess you're right," said Josh. "I should go talk to him."

Brooke's eyes widened. "You mean the What If? was about Matt?"

"Brooke . . ." Josh began. "Oh, never mind." He jumped off the yard gym and went after Matt.

Josh's bedroom window opened onto the front porch roof, a flat, shingled rectangle bordered by a low, wooden railing painted white. Josh found Matt sitting there with his back leaning against the house and Widgett crawling up his shirt front. Josh climbed out to join him.

"I've been looking for you."

Matt ignored him.

Josh sighed. "Look, I'm sorry. We all are."

"Why?"

"We thought we hurt your feelings."

"Well, you thought wrong."

"Oh."

"And, anyway, what do you care?"

"It's like I said," Josh told him. "I want to be friends with you, but . . ." Josh didn't finish.

"But I'm too stupid."

"But you keep making me mad!"

"It's not my fault you don't want me here."

"Nothing's ever your fault, is it?"

"Leave me alone."

"See, that's what really makes me mad. You can't even admit when something's your fault!"

"I wasn't bothering you, so just go away and leave me alone!"

That night the contest of the verses ended. Josh couldn't remember a thing after "every evil practice" and Matt was declared the winner. After supper, Matt went outside and Josh went into the living room to talk to his dad.

"I can't do it," he said. "I've tried to like Matt but I just can't."

"And why would that be, do you think?" asked his dad.

"He makes me so mad all the time."

"Maybe it's green you're seeing, and not the red of being angry."

"Green?"

"Jealousy, son, that old green-eyed monster."

Every evil practice, thought Josh, and he mumbled, "I'm not jealous."

"Not even just a little?"

"I don't feel jealous," said Josh, "but I keep thinking about that verse Mom gave me."

"It's God talking to you, then."

"It is?"

"The Bible is God's Word, Josh, and when your mind fastens on a verse and won't let it go, you can be pretty sure God's trying to tell you something."

With a crash and the tinkle of shattered glass, Josh's new skateboard came sailing through the front window and landed, upside down and wheels spinning, at Josh's feet. Seconds later, the front door opened and Matt rushed in.

"I didn't . . . It wasn't my f . . ." he began, but the look on Josh's face stopped him. "I'm sorry," he said. "I was trying to jump the steps like Josh does and it slipped."

"And did you take the skateboard without asking Josh?"

"No," Josh said quickly, "I let him take it."

Matt shot him a confused look, and hung his head. "I can't pay for the window," he said. "I don't have any money."

"At least you understand you *should* pay for it," said Josh's dad.

"Yes, sir." Then, looking at Josh, Matt added, "It was my fault."

"Well, then, I'll do the paying," said Josh's dad, "but you'll have to do the work of fixing the window."

"I don't know how," said Matt.

"I can show you," offered Josh.

His dad laughed. "Josh has fixed more than one broken window in his lifetime," he told Matt.

Josh picked up his skateboard by one wheel and shook glittering slivers of glass onto the braided rug. "We can start by cleaning up all this mess."

Josh's dad went to the hardware store while Josh and Matt swept and vacuumed every splinter of glass from the living room rug. After they finished, Josh showed Matt how to remove the wood frame and clean the channels for the new sheet of glass. When Josh's dad got back with the supplies, Matt was ready to putty and replace the glass and reframe the window. The job was soon done.

"I did it!" said Matt.

"That you did," said Josh's dad.

"I mean, Josh had to help me, but . . ."

"But you did the work," finished Josh.

When they returned the tools to the workshop, Matt asked, "Why'd you do it?"

"Do what?"

"Tell your dad you let me take the skate-board."

"Oh." Josh picked up a vice-grip and spun the screw. "I figured you were in enough trouble with the window."

"Yeah. Well, I mean, thanks."

"OK." Josh tossed the vice-grip back in the toolbox. "You know, you're really lousy on a skateboard."

"I know."

Josh tried not to show the surprise he felt. He never in a million years expected Matt to admit there was anything he couldn't do, especially if it was something Josh could do well. Maybe there was hope for his cousin, after all. Maybe . . .

"Maybe I could, you know, teach you some stuff."

Matt grinned. "OK."

A few minutes later Matt was riding up and down the driveway while Josh coached him from the front yard. By the time Josh's mom called them inside, Matt was showing a lot more control.

"You're doing great," Josh told him.

"Really?"

"Yeah."

"Thanks. Guess I just needed somebody to show me how."

"How come Will never showed you?"

They were at the back steps and Matt hesitated before opening the door. "Will doesn't like me, either," he said finally.

"But he's your brother," said Josh. Josh didn't have any brothers, but he always thought they sort of had to do things with you, like your parents.

"So what?" said Matt. "You're my cousin, and you don't like me."

"I like you."

"You do?"

"Yeah, I do." And, at that moment, he really did.

Chapter Seven

On Sunday, Mr. Sparks announced a lock-out for the following Friday.

"What's a lock-out?"

"It's like a lock-in," said Josh, "but we sleep outside."

Matt frowned. "So what's a lock-in?"

"Doesn't your youth group do lock-ins?"

"We don't have a youth group 'til seventh grade."

"How come?"

Matt shrugged.

"Anyway, it's when you spend the night at the church. The high school kids get to lock-in all the time. Mr. Sparks only lets us do it after we've begged him for about a year."

"Why do you want to spend the night at the church?"

"It's fun."

"What do you do?"

"Play games, mostly, and eat. We stay up all night."

"I guess you do if you have to sleep outside!"

Josh laughed. "We have sleeping bags, and Mr. Sparks has a lodge tent from when he was a Scout leader."

"But what about Widgett?"

"Mom can take care of her."

Matt held the guinea pig up to his face and she twitched her whiskers against his nose. "She'll miss me."

"It's only one night."

"What if my mom calls?"

"She won't." Aunt Harriet called Matt once a week, always on Sunday afternoon.

"But what if she does?"

"Suit yourself," Josh sighed, "but I'm going."

"I didn't say I wasn't going."

Josh liked the lock-outs better than the lock-ins. There was a two-acre patch of woods behind the parking lot at the church where they set up their tent and built a campfire. Late at night, when the moon went down and darkness closed in, six boys and Mr. Sparks huddled together around the fire. Josh sat with his back to the lights of the church and pretended he was deep in the forest.

"Who's got a story?" asked Mr. Sparks.

It had to be a Bible story, and you had to tell it without names so the others could guess who you were talking about.

"There's this guy," said Jeremy Westover, "and he's in love with this girl, but their families don't like each other so they won't let this guy and girl get married."

"That's Romeo and Juliet," said Josh. "They're not even in the Bible!"

"OK, forget the part about the families. They want to get married, and so they get engaged. But before the wedding this girl finds out she's going to have a baby. Now, the guy *knows* he's not the one . . ."

"Mary and Joseph," interrupted Josh.

"No fair," complained Jeremy. "I didn't finish yet."

"You didn't have to," said Josh.

Mr. Sparks laughed. "OK, Josh, you tell us one."

"OK," said Josh slowly, stalling for time to think. "There was this guy . . ."

"We already heard that one," said Matt, and everyone laughed.

"It's another guy," said Josh, "and he had eight sons. And they were all really good-looking and had really important jobs. Three of them were in the army. I don't know what the others did, except the youngest one watched the sheep."

"Oh, yeah," said Matt sarcastically, "that's a real important job."

"Actually it was," said Mr. Sparks. "The tribes depended on sheep for food and wool, and it was the shepherd's job to keep the flock together and protect it from wild animals."

"It's the boy who cried wolf!" said Jeremy.

"That's not in the Bible, either," said Josh.

"Anyway, this kid was really good at his job, but he was kind of weird. He used to sit around and make up songs all the time."

"What's so weird about that?" asked Jeremy.

"OK, so he wasn't weird," said Josh, "but nobody paid much attention to him because he was always hanging out with the sheep."

"Now, that's weird!" said Matt, and everyone laughed.

Josh punched Matt's arm and gave him a warning look.

Mr. Sparks said, "OK, Josh, we have eight brothers and one was a shepherd. What happened next?"

"OK, so there was this really famous judge, and he went to the house one day and told this guy that one of his sons was going to be the next king of Israel."

"Have they got kings in Israel?" asked Bobby Lightner.

"They did then," said Mr. Sparks.

"So the guy got all his sons," continued Josh, "except the one that was out with the sheep, and showed them to the judge. But the judge shook his head and asked the guy if he had any more sons, and the guy said yeah he did but he was just a kid."

"Sounds like Cinderella," said Jeremy.

Josh ignored him. "Well, the judge asked to see the kid, and so the guy sent one of his sons to take care of the sheep so the kid could come home and meet the judge. And as soon as he walked in, the judge said, 'That's him! He's going to be the next king of Israel.'"

"Just like Cinderella," said Jeremy.

"It's not Cinderella," said Josh. "It's a real story from the Bible."

"Anybody know who the kid was?" asked Mr. Sparks.

Bobby punched Jeremy, who punched Matt, who giggled, but didn't say anything.

"Nobody?" asked Mr. Sparks. "Kenny?"

Kenny Stratford smiled nervously and looked at Josh. Josh grinned. Kenny always knew the answer but never thought he did.

"I don't know. Was it David?"

"Right!" said Mr. Sparks. "Thank you, Josh, that was a good one. OK, Kenny, it's your turn."

Kenny started his story and Josh knew it was about Daniel, but he didn't say anything. When

it was time to guess, he leaned over and whispered the answer to Matt.

"Daniel!" said Matt.

"Good," said Mr. Sparks. "OK, Matt, your turn."

"I haven't got one," said Matt.

"You gave the answer," said Mr. Sparks. "Now you have to tell a story. We'll give you a minute to think of one."

Matt glared at Josh through the firelight. Josh had only been trying to help, but it looked like he had set Matt up.

"I don't know any," Matt admitted grudgingly.

"It's getting late, anyway," said Mr. Sparks.

There were groans around the campfire, directed at Matt. Matt glared at Josh again. Josh felt guilty and tried to think of a way to prove to Matt he hadn't done it on purpose.

"We didn't sing yet," he suggested.

"Nice try, Josh," said Mr. Sparks, "but we're all tired. Let's just have a prayer and hit the sleeping bags."

"You said you stayed up all night," hissed Matt.

"We do," whispered Josh, "just not on purpose."

Mr. Sparks asked them to join hands for the prayer, but Matt snatched his away when Josh tried to hold it. After the prayer, Josh said, "Look, I'm sorry, OK?"

"No, you're not. You did it on purpose to make me look stupid."

"Did not. I was trying to help."

"Now everybody's mad at me, and it's all your fault."

"It's your fault, too. I just gave you the answer. I didn't make you say it."

Matt frowned. "OK, so maybe it wasn't *all* your fault."

Josh stared. He did it again! For the second time in a week, Matt admitted something was his own fault.

"How do you know so many Bible stories?" asked Matt.

"How come you don't?" asked Josh. "You know lots of verses."

"Yeah, but I didn't know all those stories were in there."

"What did you think the verses were?"

Matt shrugged. "Just verses."

Josh frowned. He had never thought of the verses all by themselves, just like Matt had never thought of them all put together into stories. It reminded him of one of those hidden picture puzzles that was one thing if you just looked at it, and a whole bunch of other things if you looked really close.

Mr. Sparks put his sleeping bag across the door of the tent and pretended to stay awake while the boys whispered and punched one another and giggled and pretended to be asleep. Josh thought Matt dozed off a couple of times, but he wasn't sure. He knew he didn't sleep all night. He was thinking about Bible verses and remembering how that one verse had stuck with him. As his dad said, his mind had fastened on it and wouldn't let it go.

When they got home, Josh and Matt went to bed and slept until the middle of the afternoon. They would have slept all day, but Josh's mom fixed a late lunch and made them get up to eat it.

"I'm not hungry," Josh mumbled into his pillow.

"You will be, once you're up. Come on now, or you won't be able to sleep tonight."

Matt got up and went to Widgett's cage. "I'm starving," he said, taking her into his hands. "How about you, Widgett?"

Josh's mom laughed. "She's been stuffing herself ever since you got home this morning."

Matt smiled and put the guinea pig back through the trapdoor. "Thanks for taking care of her."

"I told you she'd be OK," said Josh, sitting on the side of his bed and staring at his feet. When his mom made a little startled gasp, he looked up. She was looking at the window, and Mr. Peepers was looking back.

Matt jumped in front of Widgett's cage and squealed, "Make him go away!"

"I'll get him," said Josh, but when he went to the window Mr. Peepers took off across the roof. Josh opened the window.

"Don't you dare!" said his mom.

"What?"

"Don't you dare go out on the roof after that cat!"

"OK," said Josh reluctantly, as he grabbed his

jeans. "I'll get dressed and go tell Mrs. Jenson he's out."

"I'll *call* Mrs. Jenson," said his mom. "You eat your lunch."

Matt ate lunch in his pajamas. When he was finished he started upstairs to dress. "Wait for me," he told Josh.

Josh kicked impatiently at the back door. "OK, but hurry."

Just as his mom said, "Don't kick the door, Josh," they heard Matt scream.

Josh and his mom raced upstairs. Matt was standing in the middle of the room gazing in horror at the guinea pig cage. Widgett was gone!

Chapter Eight

How did she get out?" asked Josh.

His mom went quickly to the window and closed it. "Don't worry. She's around here somewhere."

Matt was in tears. "No, she's not! The cat ate her!"

"Mr. Peepers wouldn't do that," said Josh.

"Yes, he would. You said so!"

Josh tried not to notice his mom frowning at him. "It was a joke."

"You left the window open on purpose," accused Matt, "so he could get in."

"You know that's not true," said Josh's mom, putting her arm around Matt's shoulders.

Josh knew it, too, but he had left the window open when he knew Mr. Peepers was out. He looked at his mom. "You think Mr. Peepers did eat Widgett?"

"Of course not! If that cat had been in here, there would be evidence. The cage would be turned over for one thing."

Josh looked at the cage. "Yeah! Matt probably just left the trapdoor open and she got out."

"I didn't leave the trapdoor open."

"You were upset," said Josh's mom. "Maybe you didn't quite get it closed all the way."

"I closed it," said Matt. "I know I did."

Josh and his mom helped Matt search the room, the upstairs, and finally, the downstairs. Josh even climbed out on the porch roof. They searched the rest of the afternoon, but Widgett was still nowhere to be found. Matt wouldn't go down for supper, so Josh took him a sandwich.

"I'm not hungry."

"That's OK. You can eat it later."

"Just leave me alone."

Josh didn't know what to say until he remembered something from the Bible. "Jesus said God takes care of animals," he told Matt.

"Did not."

"Did so. He said God even cares about the sparrows."

"Are not two sparrows sold for a penny?"

"What?"

"That's the verse. 'Yet not one of them will fall to the ground apart from the will of your Father.' Matthew 10:29."

"Yeah, that's it!"

"So what?"

Josh frowned. How could Matt know the verse and not understand what it meant? "Well, it's what He told the apostles, you know, when He sent them out to heal people and stuff. He meant they didn't have to worry because God was going to take care of them."

"What's that got to do with Widgett?"

"Well, shoot, if He knows when a bird falls, don't you think He knows when a guinea pig's lost?"

Matt's eyes filled with tears. "But she's not lost. She's . . . She's . . ."

"No, she isn't," said Josh. "Like Mom said, she's around here somewhere, and we'll find her."

Matt wiped his eyes. "You don't understand. She wouldn't run away from me. She loves me. She's the only one who does."

Josh stared. "But . . . your mom loves you, and your dad . . ."

"Then why did they send me away?"

Josh was confused. "You mean here? Your mom was sick."

"I could have helped."

"But she's not even home."

"I could have gotten a job, like Will."

Josh thought a minute. "Well, I don't know. But it doesn't mean they don't love you."

"Everyone's helping but me," said Matt. "At least Widgett needed me, and now she's gone."

"You still think it was my fault?"

Matt looked at his hands. "I think it was my fault. Mr. Peepers couldn't have gotten her if the trapdoor was closed all the way."

Josh looked at the cage. "I don't think he could get her if the trapdoor was wide open."

"Why not?"

"Well, just look at this thing. All she'd have to do is crawl up under that bottom shelf and he wouldn't be able to reach her."

Hope shone in Matt's eyes. "He'd have to tear the whole cage apart to get her!"

"Mom's right. Mr. Peepers probably wasn't even in here."

Josh grinned broadly, but Matt frowned and his lip quivered. "Then she did run away from me."

"Maybe she's just exploring."

"And she went outside, all by herself."

"We'll find her. We'll get the kids to help."

"And Mr. Peepers probably ate her after all, before Mrs. Jenson could catch him."

Josh sighed.

"Why couldn't she keep her stupid cat inside," said Matt. "It's all her fault, the old . . ."

Matt was crying again.

"The old crow," suggested Josh helplessly.

The next afternoon Josh got the kids together for a guinea pig search. Matt was convinced they were wasting their time.

"You need to stay inside, anyway," said Josh, "until your mom calls."

They divided up into pairs. Marty and Georgie checked the bushes around Josh's house. Michael and Erin checked the workshop, while Brooke and Megan checked the garage. Josh went to check the sandbox in Megan's backyard. Nobody found Widgett.

"She's got to be somewhere," said Josh as they gathered on his patio.

"Maybe she's still in the house," suggested Erin.

"We already looked."

"She's so little," said Megan, "she could be anywhere."

"Maybe she'll come back by herself," said Brooke.

"If she can," said Josh.

"What do you mean?"

"Matt thinks Mr. Peepers got her."

Erin gasped. "He wouldn't!"

"That's what I said," Josh told her, "but what if he did?"

"Well, he wouldn't," said Erin, "but if he did Aunt Jody would get Matt another guinea pig."

"I don't want another guinea pig." Matt was coming from the kitchen with a pitcher of lemonade and some paper cups. "I told you you wouldn't find her."

"We'll find her." Josh took the pitcher and poured the lemonade.

Brooke said, "There's no place else to look."

"Then we'll just have to look in the same places again," said Megan, glancing at Matt.

Matt went back inside and they drank their lemonade in silence. When they were finished they fanned out to check the yard again. Josh followed Megan into the workshop.

"Matt's really upset, isn't he?" she asked.

"Widgett's been gone a whole day."

"Are you sure she's not in the house, Josh?"

"We looked everywhere."

"But even if she did go out the window, how could a guinea pig get down from the roof?"

Josh shrugged. "Same way Mr. Peepers got up there, I guess."

"But she's so little."

"Megan?"

"What?"

"The Bible says if you ask for something you'll get it."

"I know. 'Ask, and it will be given to you.'"

"Yeah. Well, do you think it would be OK if we, you know, ask for Widgett to come back?"

"You mean pray?"

"Yeah, I guess."

"I already did."

Josh figured if Megan thought it was OK to pray for a guinea pig, then it must be, so while he helped her search the workshop, he prayed, *Help us find Widgett, God. Please? And take care of her until we do. Jesus said you would. Amen. Thanks. Amen.*

Nobody found Widgett. They drank the rest of the lemonade, and then everyone went home, except Erin.

"Mr. Peepers didn't do it." she said.

Josh didn't answer.

"Aunt Jody had a parakeet once and it kept getting out of its cage. Mr. Peepers never even paid any attention to it."

"Parakeets can fly," said Josh.

"But this one used to drink out of Mr. Peepers'

water bowl. There were plenty of times he could have caught it, but he didn't."

Josh looked at Erin. She had a point. And he never really thought Mr. Peepers was guilty, anyway. But there was no way to prove it until they found Widgett. "We've got to find that guinea pig," he said.

"Maybe Aunt Jody could help."

"No offense," said Josh doubtfully, "but I've seen her try to catch Mr. Peepers."

"This is different. Aunt Jody knows a lot about where Widgett would go."

"That's a great idea, Erin! Sort of a Sherlock Holmes for guinea pigs!"

Erin laughed. "Better not say that to Aunt Jody!"

They went through the house to see if Matt wanted to go with them, but they didn't find him.

"He went out a half hour ago," said Josh's dad. "Right after he talked to his mom. I thought he'd be with you."

Josh shrugged and opened the front door. What he saw outside stopped him in his tracks. "Dad, I think you'd better come here."

Chapter Nine

Mrs. Jenson marched Matt across the street and up the front walk. Josh, Erin, and Josh's dad lined up on the porch to watch them.

"Go ahead," said Mrs. Jenson, positioning Matt in front of his uncle. "Tell him what you did."

Matt hung his head.

"What's this about, Matt?" asked Josh's dad.

Matt mumbled something.

"Look at me, son, and tell me clear."

Matt lifted his chin. "I tore up her roses."

"Now why in God's green earth would you want to do a thing like that?"

There were tears standing in Matt's eyes, but his mouth was a firm, straight line as he faced Josh's dad in silence.

"You see?" said Mrs. Jenson. "He admits to kicking down the trellis, but he won't say why. I just don't understand."

Josh understood.

His dad sighed. "Well, let's go survey the damage."

As they started off the porch, Josh held Erin back. "I think I know why he did it," he told her, keeping his voice low.

"Because of Mr. Peepers?" asked Erin.

Josh nodded, watching the others. When they were nearly to the street, he and Erin followed.

"But that's all wrong!"

"I know," said Josh, "but it's what he thinks."

"I have to tell her."

"OK, but let me talk to Matt first."

Erin nodded, then sighed. "I sure wish we could've found that guinea pig."

Josh did, too. Mrs. Jenson's beautiful pink and red roses were smashed and scattered across her side yard. The white, fan-shaped trellis that had held them against the house lay in splintered pieces among the fallen blossoms.

Josh watched his dad's face grow red and he waited for the explosion. It didn't come. When his dad spoke, his voice was hushed and determined.

"This is one time you'll have to face the music on your own, Matt. You'll be expected to pay for what you've done."

"I haven't got any money," said Matt simply.

"Then you'll work if off, if that's agreeable to Mrs. Jenson."

"I won't work for her."

"You will, mister, and that's an end to it."

"No, sir, I won't."

Josh held his breath. The muscle in his dad's jaw rippled and his bushy eyebrows sank toward the bridge of his nose. "I'll have an explanation from you, young man," he told Matt, "and I'll have it now!"

Matt remained silent.

"He thinks Mr. Peepers ate his guinea pig," said Erin.

"What!" Mrs. Jenson's eyes grew large behind the round lenses of her glasses.

"The boy's guinea pig turned up missing yesterday," explained Josh's dad.

"And my cat was out yesterday," said Mrs. Jenson.

"But it's not true!" said Erin. "Peeps wouldn't hurt Widgett."

Josh's dad fixed his gaze on Matt and spoke firmly. "Even if it were true, Matt, you're wrong to be taking it out on Mrs. Jenson."

"She let him get out," said Matt.

Josh pulled back without thinking, stepping away from Matt as if he expected lightning to strike at any moment. His dad's big, gentle hands curled themselves into fists and then released again.

"Go to your room," he told Matt. "You're grounded."

Matt mutely obeyed. Turning to watch him go, Josh noticed his mom standing on their front porch, arms crossed in front of her, waiting. Josh sighed.

"I can help clean this up," he offered.

Mrs. Jenson smiled at him. His dad gave him a pat on the back and said, "I'll help, too. And, of course, we'll want to pay for the damage."

"Not just yet," said Mrs. Jenson. "Let's give Matt a couple of days to change his mind."

Josh didn't see Matt again until supper, when no mention was made of guinea pigs, cats, roses, or trellises. After supper, Josh took his skateboard and went outside for a while, but he couldn't keep his mind on one-eighties and figure eights. Finally, he went to his room. Matt was lying on the bed staring at the ceiling.

"Hi."

Matt didn't answer.

"Boy, you really did it this time."

Matt turned on his side, putting his back toward Josh.

Josh kicked at Matt's clothes, which were strewn across the floor. "Oh, man, look what you did to my room!" Using the side of his foot, he slid a pair of jeans in the general direction of Matt's bed. "It looks worse than those old roses in Mrs. Jenson's yard."

"Just shut up."

"He can talk!" exclaimed Josh cheerfully.

Matt turned over. "Shut up!"

"But he can only say one thing."

"Go away," said Matt, fighting back a smile.

Josh gasped in mock surprise. "It's a major scientific breakthrough!"

Matt giggled. "Leave me alone."

"OK," said Josh, "but you'll be begging me to hang around after you've been grounded for about six weeks."

"You're joking, right? He won't give me that much time."

"I don't know. He was pretty mad."

"Yeah, but six weeks?" Matt sat up, crossing his legs under him.

"Well, I figured he'd kill you, so I guess you're lucky you're just grounded."

"Six weeks," said Matt. "That's the whole rest of the summer."

"He'd let you off if you told Mrs. Jenson . . ."

"No."

Josh kicked a T-shirt toward Matt's bed and picked another one off his desk using the tips of his thumb and his forefinger. "Yuck."

"It's just a T-shirt."

"There's a sandwich under there."

"You brought it up here," Matt reminded him. "Last night."

Josh examined the sandwich closely. The top piece of bread was gone and most of the lettuce was missing. The ham hadn't been touched. "You have a funny way of eating a sandwich."

"I didn't eat it. I wasn't hungry, remember?"

Suddenly Matt jumped up and ran to the desk. He picked up the remaining bit of lettuce and pointed to a jagged crescent in the edge of it. "Look! Teeth marks."

"Widgett?" asked Josh.

Matt nodded, grinning from ear to ear. "She's alive!"

"Mr. Peepers is innocent!"

Matt's smile faded. "And I smashed Mrs. Jenson's roses for nothing."

"You're going to be her slave for the rest of the summer," said Josh.

"You think Erin's mad at me?"

Josh gave Matt a shrewd, sideways look. "You like Erin?"

"No! I just don't want her to be mad at me, that's all."

"Matt likes Erin, Matt likes Erin," sang Josh.

"Do not!"

"Do so."

"Do not!"

"OK, OK," said Josh, then mumbled, "Do so."

Matt threw a pillow at him. Josh laughed and fell back onto his bed. Matt frowned. "But where could she be?"

Josh propped up on his elbows. "Who? Erin?"

"No, stupid, Widgett."

"Oh, yeah. Stupid Widgett."

Matt gave him a disgusted look and Josh tossed the pillow back at him.

"I mean it," said Matt. "We've already looked every place we could think of. So where can she be?"

Josh sat up and looked around the room. Matt's things were scattered everywhere. "About a dozen guinea pigs could be hiding in this mess!"

Matt pulled his suitcase out from under the bed and dumped its contents in the middle of the floor.

"Oh, yeah," said Josh, "that helps a lot!"

Matt spread the suitcase open on the bed and

checked every pocket. He started picking up his clothes piece by piece, checking all the pockets before tossing them into the suitcase.

"I get it!" said Josh, and helped him.

Ten minutes later the suitcase was full, but there was still no sign of Widgett. "At least I got my room cleaned," said Josh.

Matt closed the suitcase and shoved it back under the bed. "Now what?" he asked, leaning against the headboard and stretching his legs out in front of him. Josh did the same on his own bed and they both surveyed the room with their eyes.

Josh spotted the sandwich. "Maybe we should just wait for her to get hungry again."

Maybe, but that bread and lettuce will last her a long time."

"I bet she's thirsty."

Matt jumped up, refilled Widgett's water dish at the bathroom sink, and put it on the desk next to the sandwich. Then he went back to his position on the bed.

Josh watched the desk. He look at Matt, who was watching the desk. Josh sighed. "Well, this is fun."

"You don't have to stay."

"Maybe I won't," said Josh, swinging his legs off the side of the bed. But he heard his dad's footsteps on the stairs and said, "Maybe I will."

Matt sat up, too, and waited. Josh's dad came into the room and looked at Matt. "Well? Do you think maybe we can talk about this thing now?"

"Yes, sir."

"And do you see that what you did was wrong?"

"Yes, sir, and I'll work for Mrs. Jenson to pay for it."

Josh nearly laughed at the surprised look on his dad's face. "Widgett's alive," he told him. "She ate some of Matt's sandwich."

He nodded toward the desk, then stared in disbelief. There sat Widgett drinking placidly from her water dish, and no one had seen where she had come from.

Chapter Ten

Matt jumped to his feet, but Josh stopped him. "Wait," he whispered.

"Why?"

"Shh. I don't know about you, but I want to see where she goes."

"Oh." Matt nodded and waited.

They all waited. It was so quiet that the ticking of Josh's alarm clock sounded like the chimes from the church bells on Sunday mornings. It was *too* quiet. Widgett raised her head and looked at them. She walked to the front of the desk, stood on her hind legs, and sniffed at them. Josh held his breath. Widgett went back to her water bowl.

"Whew," said Josh, letting his breath out slowly.

"She knows we're here," whispered Matt. "Can't I . . . ?"

"No."

Widgett finished drinking and sniffed at the sandwich. The she waddled across to the desk and sniffed around her cage. Josh's dad shoved his hands into his pockets and shifted to the other foot. Widgett looked at him.

"Looks like she's come home," he said softly. "I don't think she's going back."

"Me neither," whispered Matt.

Widgett looked at the door as Josh's mom hurried into the room. "What's going on up here? Is everything . . ."

Josh's dad held up his hand to stop her, then pointed to the desk. "Widgett!" she cried happily and had the guinea pig cradled in her hands before anyone could say another word.

"Mom!" complained Josh.

"What?"

Matt rushed to take Widgett. Josh's dad put an arm around his wife's shoulders. "We were watching to see if she'd give away her hiding place."

"Oh. Sorry."

"No harm. Matt and I think she was home to stay."

"She is now," said Josh unhappily.

Matt put some food in her cage and replaced the water dish. When he lowered Widgett through the trapdoor though, she ignored the food, climbed the ramps and ladders, and pulled herself back out. The she disappeared behind the desk before anyone could react.

Josh's dad winked at him. "Help me with this," he said, moving to one end of the desk. Josh took the other end, and they carefully moved the desk away from the wall.

Widgett had made a nest in the space beneath the bottom drawer on the left-hand side. She had stolen two socks and the front cover off a paperback book. Nestled in the shredded cardboard looking like miniature Widgetts were four baby guinea pigs.

"Widgett's a mommy!" exclaimed Matt.

"How did she do that?" asked Josh.

His dad laughed his deep, bellowing laugh and Josh blushed. "I didn't mean, you know, how," he stammered. "I mean, she's pretty special, but not even Widgett can have babies all by herself!"

His mom came to his rescue. "Well, I think it's a very good question."

Matt thought about it. "We had Pet Circus the last week of school," he said finally. "Widgett won the guinea pig race."

Josh's dad said, "There it is. The daddy was most likely one of the other contestants."

Josh grinned and squatted next to the nest. The pups were tiny, but they looked like scaled-down versions of grown-up guinea pigs, like his model race cars. "They've got hair and teeth and everything!"

"Guinea pigs don't have much time to be babies," explained his mom.

Two were black and white, like Widgett. One was mostly white with black feet, and one was brown with white around its face and down its chest. "I like that one," said Josh, pointing to the brown one but being careful not to touch it.

"You want him?" asked Matt.

Josh stood up. "You mean it?"

Matt nodded and Josh looked at his dad. His dad looked at Josh's mom. His mom frowned. "Please, Mom?" begged Josh. "You said, yourself, that Widgett wasn't any trouble."

"I was talking about one night."

"Please?"

His mom looked at Widgett's four nursing babies, and the corners of her mouth turned up. It wasn't quite a smile, but Josh knew he had won. He gave her an enthusiastic hug and kissed her cheek. "Thanks, Mom!"

"I didn't say yes," she protested.

"But you will, right?"

Finally she smiled. "We'll see."

Josh whooped. Widgett raised her head and looked at him. Matt said, "Shh. You'll scare the babies."

Josh's mom helped Matt get Widgett and her new family settled safely into the cage. "Why did she run away like that?" he asked her.

"Animals just do that sometimes when they're going to have babies. I guess it makes them feel safe."

"But she was safe with me," said Matt. "I thought she loved me."

Josh thought of Aunt Harriet and how Matt felt left out of his family's problems. Now even Widgett was leaving him out of things.

"It was something she needed to do by herself," said Josh's mom. "That doesn't mean she doesn't love you."

"She came back, didn't she?" Josh reminded him.

"Of course, she did," said his mom. "Now, you boys get to bed. It's late."

When the lights were out and the rest of the house was sleeping, Josh stared into the darkness thinking about cousins and guinea pigs.

"Matt?" he whispered. "You asleep?"

"Yeah. I mean, no."

"I'm glad Widgett's back."

"Me, too."

"I can't wait to show the kids her babies."

"Yeah, they're pretty cool."

"Especially the brown one."

Matt giggled. "I mean your friends."

"Oh. Yeah, they're OK."

"They all came over to look for Widgett. That's pretty cool."

"It was, wasn't it?" Josh propped up on one elbow. "What's that verse? You know, where they're talking about the church? Something about all for one and one for all."

"Wasn't that The Three Musketeers?"

Josh giggled. "That's not what it *says*, it's just what it means. It's the one Dad gave you, about suffering."

"Suffer the little children"?

"Just forget it."

"Oh, I know! 'If one part suffers, every part suffers with it; if one part is honored, every part rejoices with it.' 1 Corinthians 12:26."

"That's it! If one suffers, they all suffer. That's the way the Grace Street Kids are."

"Kind of like a family."

"Yeah, I guess."

"Except not my family."

"You really think they don't love you?"

"I don't know. I guess they do. They just don't want me around."

Josh sighed and lay back down. He thought about the Bible. There was an answer in there somewhere. Mr. Sparks said there always was. Josh was almost asleep when he remembered something he needed to do. *Thanks, God,* he prayed. *For Widgett, I mean. Amen.*

In the morning, Matt barely touched his breakfast, and Josh knew he was worried about facing Mrs. Jenson.

"You want me to go with you?"

Matt looked with hope at Josh's mom.

"I don't see why not," she said.

Josh grinned. "She'll probably just yell at you and stuff today. She probably won't beat you until she's gotten some work out of you."

"Josh!" His mom tried to look stern. "Mrs. Jenson is a sweet, gentle person. I don't know why you can't make more of an effort to get along with her."

"Matt's going to be making an effort, that's for sure!"

His mom turned her back and went to the sink, but Josh could tell she was smiling. Matt looked like he was trying to smile but was just too scared. Josh grinned at him.

"It's a joke, man."

"Yeah. Maybe!"

Mrs. Jenson was sweeping her front porch as Matt and Josh came across the yard. When they reached the steps, she stopped and leaned on her broom.

"Hello, boys."

"Hi," said Josh.

Matt shoved his hands in his pockets and turned red. Mrs. Jenson smiled pleasantly and waited. Matt coughed.

"He's going to say he's sorry," said Josh, "when he gets through being embarrassed."

Mrs. Jenson put a hand to her mouth and ducked her head. Matt leaned into Josh's side and poked him in the ribs with his elbow. Josh laughed.

"I'm sorry, too," said Mrs. Jenson, "about your guinea pig."

"Oh, she came back," said Josh.

"She did? That's wonderful!"

"She had four babies," said Matt.

"She had babies?"

Matt nodded. "I'm sorry I accused Mr. Peepers of . . . you know. And I'm real sorry I tore up your roses."

"I accept your apology. Do you think we can be friends now?"

"I guess so."

"Good. How about you, Josh?"

"Me?"

"Yes, you. I'd like for us to be friends, as well. Do you think we could?"

It was Josh's turn to blush as he mumbled, "Sure."

"Then, I'll tell you what. As your friend, I'll allow you to skateboard in my driveway."

Josh was so surprised he forgot his embarrassment. "You will?"

"Yes, and as *my* friend, you'll make sure the wheels don't go off the edges and chip the concrete. Agreed?"

"Agreed."

"Good. Then it's all settled." She smiled at Josh, then turned to Matt. "I was going to set out some new roses this afternoon. Would you like to help me?"

"OK."

"I'm help, too," said Josh.

"Thank you, Josh," said Mrs. Jenson, "but this is a two-person job."

"Oh."

Mrs. Jenson laughed. "Don't look so disappointed. 'They also serve who only stand and wait,' you know."

Josh brightened. "Yeah! Like, if your mom's sick and you have to go to your cousin's 'til she's better."

Mrs. Jenson glanced at Matt. "That's one example."

"So you'd really be helping, even if you didn't feel like you were doing anything."

Mrs. Jenson smiled and Josh knew she understood. "You'd be helping a lot," she said, "because your mom wouldn't have to worry about you, on top of everything else."

"You think so?" asked Matt.

"I'm sure of it."

Matt looked doubtful.

"Besides," said Josh, "the way you eat, they're saving gobs of money just not having to feed you!"

Matt grinned.

"The Bible says we each contribute with our own special gifts," said Mrs. Jenson, "and no one's contribution is any less important than anyone else's."

"The Bible says that?" asked Matt.

"In 1 Corinthians," said Josh. "About the gifts of the Spirit." It was the answer he had been trying to think of.

Matt smiled happily. "You want to see Widgett's babies?" he asked Mrs. Jenson.

"I'd love to! Just let me call Erin."

Mrs. Jenson went inside and told Erin the good news. Erin called the Allens, then Brooke called Megan, and Georgie called Marty. They all met in Josh's room to look at the baby guinea pigs. Matt and Widgett were the center of attention, but Josh didn't mind. He watched the chocolate brown pup with the fuzzy white face and decided it was turning into a pretty good summer after all, in spite of his cousin and guinea pigs.